Beware Us Flowers of the Devil

Alexander Zelenyj

2nd Edition
Limited to 100 copies

Beware Us Flowers of the Devil
by Alexander Zelenyj

2nd Edition
Limited to 100 copies

Originally published as an exclusive edition only available as a free gift with preorders of the author's collection *Beware Us Flowers of the Annihilator*

Cover Art by David Rix based on the images:

The dun deer wooed with manner bland, And cowered beneath her lily hand. 1920, by Warwick Goble

Atomic Explosion, 1951, from the US Airforce

Publication Date: September 2025

Table of Contents

Author's Note: Four Fires

The first story in this limited edition chapbook, "The Boy and the Devil", is my retelling of an old Norwegian folktale. The setting has changed, being more Canadianized, which came out naturally, of course. The ending of the story is vastly different though, and seems in keeping with the darker edge of a lot of folktales and fairy tales I've read, as well as with my own work.

"Joy in a World on Fire" was originally to be included in my full-length collection, *Beware Us Flowers of the Annihilator*. I decided to take it out because it's a fairly lengthy tale, and there were already a few longer pieces in the book (one novella-length, in fact), and also because its experimental structure and style seemed outside the already extensive parameters of the collection. It's one of the weirder apocalyptic stories—and one of the weirder family dramas—I've written.

The third story here, "There is Only One", is an old story that I came across while digging through my files. It just slithered its way into this chapbook and I decided to leave it where it had decided to go.

The fourth story, "Gods and Devils and Those Caught Between", was written in a flash of inspiration and adds a touch of twisted hopefulness into an otherwise dark and bleak collection. It also fits, thematically, and seems an appropriately weird way to end this weird and scarce little volume.

- AZ

The Boy and the Devil

Once upon a time on a bright June morning, a boy walked down a dusty county road, cracking black walnuts as he went. He found one nut with a worm-hole in it, hollowed out, its fruit long since eaten by a larva. The boy was about to toss the useless nut into the grass when all at once, in a pearl of smoke and with a stink of shit in the air, the Devil appeared, blocking the road.

"Greetings, child," the Devil said. He was smiling, showing the boy his sharp long fangs.

The boy stared at the Beast, a shudder in his heart. The great curved horns scratching at the branches overhead, the cloven hooves and the red snake slithering inside his big mouth—these things frightened the boy deeply. They frightened him more than the distant smokestacks in the distant city, which all day long spit their long black clouds of smoke like tethers from the dirty world to the once-clean clouds, the sight of which always chilled the boy.

"Is it true what some say," said the boy, the idea forming in his mind even as the words spilled from his mouth, hardening his heart, "that the Devil is as great as the whole wide world, but also that he can make himself as small as he wants, even so small that he can slip through a needle's eye?"

"Yes, and yes," answered the Devil, a prideful expression settling over his raw-meat face. His snake-tongue flicked and hissed; his grotesque corpse-stench grew stronger.

"Wow! Amazing!" cried the boy. "*Please* will you let me see this, and creep inside this nut?" He held up the worm-holed nut for the Devil to see.

And the Devil did—faster than the boy could follow, the Beast became a flash of black lightning that flew into the nut. The impact staggered the boy, and the nut nearly flew from his hand. Peering at the nut in his fingers, he saw that a tiny crimson eye filled the entirety of the hole, watching him.

The boy snatched a stick from the grass and jammed it into the worm-hole. A great screeching sounded from inside the nut, muffled but unmistakably full of agony, and brimming with fury. The nut began a terrible shaking, and he had to clamp both hands around it to hold it steady. "Now I've got you!" the boy cried triumphantly.

A heaviness had fallen from his heart.

He walked on down the road and the sun shone brightly. He ignored the ugly factory smokestacks sullying the sky in the distance. He tried to ignore the shaking nut cupped in his hands.

Soon he came to the forge that lay at the edge of the town. An idea bloomed in his mind at the sight of the small brick building. He went inside and asked the smith if he might be able to crack the nut for him. "I've tried so many times but can't crack this one," the boy explained. He reasoned that if he were able to destroy the nut then the Devil inside would be destroyed, too; and then the whole world would be better off.

"That should be easy enough," said the smith, chuckling and eyeing the nut and clamping his big hands together in anticipation of what he likely thought an easy task. He removed a small hammer from his tools, laid the nut on the anvil, and hit it with the hammer. It did not crack. So he took up a larger hammer and tried again, but neither the hammer nor the strength of the blow was heavy enough to do the job. He took an even larger hammer and smote it down on the nut, but nothing, again. The smith was very angry by this time, his cheeks flushed with embarrassment.

He then got out his huge sledgehammer. "I *will* crack you yet, nut!"

He struck the nut with all his might, and the nut was finally crushed. But, uncannily, the blow caused a great roaring that filled the room, a tumult of wind and wolves howling combined, and the roof of the forge rattled and the glass in the windows grew cracks everywhere. The shards of the nut, and the branch that had blocked the nut's worm-hole, were smoking, and embers drifted in the air.

When the din quieted, the smith looked at the boy, his eyes relieved but afraid.

"I think," he said, voice quiet, "that the Devil was in that nut."

"Yes, he was!" cried the boy. He was elated—his plan had worked, and the world was better now than it had been.

He thanked the smith and left the forge, continuing homeward. As he walked, though, he realized that his heart felt burdened again, and his great joy had gone away. A nameless worry crept into his awareness, and as if mirroring his sour mood, the sun of earlier in the day had grown dimmed, hidden behind the clouds.

Uncertainty gnawed at the boy late into the night, while he lay sleepless in bed. He understood suddenly what bothered him: he feared that the trick he'd played hadn't worked as he'd planned, and that the hammer-blow from the smith hadn't vanquished the Devil at all…but freed him.

It was just as the child felt certain of his grave mistake that a single great vivid red eye appeared in the darkness.

"Tricky foolish doomed boy," said the Devil. "Now. You're. In. *My*. Prison."

Joy in a World on Fire

I: Today the Fire-Buriers

The sun was lost to the badness of the day.

The boy stood beside the old man, watching the oppressive clouds devouring the sky. The wind lashed the clothes against their bodies like a punishment. The child trembled beneath its bite while the man continued his toil in the rubble as if untouched by these invasive elements of winter bullying the dying autumn. Up went the pick and down it fell to pierce the concrete and bite into the bedrock beneath, the man's mighty arms fighting the earth and, like a miracle, winning the contest.

The boy, weary from helping the old man, held his spade in weak fingers numbed with cold, callused from the wood of the shovel. His breath was laboured and ragged, and his knees buckled beneath the gale wind. He could only watch, awed, the old man immersed in the rhythm of fighting the concrete, his arms and the pick like a great pendulum, his face set in the exertion of the task. A few minutes later, having cracked the face of the street, the old man jabbed his pick into the ground and took up the rusty-headed shovel from where it lay beside him. Without pause, he began deepening the hole he'd made, making heaps of the softer, moister soil around the hole's rim. They'd been unlucky today—many of the already open holes they'd come across had fallen victim to rockslides so that digging them again posed too great a danger. They'd been forced more often than not to dig new holes for the burial of the unholy things, and digging in the city was a formidable task.

The boy, awed by the old man's endurance, made more tired by witnessing it, took a moment and scanned the dead city before them:

Everywhere the fire-orbs hung in the air. They smouldered angrily, sending sparks spitting and sputtering down to earth. Some hung high among the dark-windowed apartment buildings and distant skyscrapers, others only a few feet from street level. The collective voice of the orbs haunted the barren city: the perpetual crackling of flames and, beneath it, an obscene humming, as if the things droned from slumbers disturbed by dark dreams.

The man worked and worked, until the top of his head disappeared beyond the hole's rim. Then, finished digging this latest hole, he appeared again, clambering up out of the earth, his features hard and dirty and sweaty. He turned to the sac of grey flaccid flesh lying on the earth beside his boot and scooped it onto the shovel. It steamed on the air, its life-heat fighting the death he'd delivered it thirty minutes before, even as he heaved it into the darkness of its burial hole. Immediately he began refilling the hole with shovel-fulls of earth, working furiously, for he knew that soon the lingering vestiges of energy in the thing would combust, as they always did within an hour of an orb's death.

Fifteen minutes later it was finished. He retrieved the long spear from beside the desiccated grass of the median strip where he'd buried a pair of the things earlier that day and nearly set off a massive landslide when one or both of the interred things had combusted and shaken the earth. "Come on, boy." His voice was hoarse. He trudged away across the crooked ground, circumventing a towering pile of rubble from which the nose of a rusted car protruded. The boy gathered his tools and scurried to follow him through the ruins.

Something caught the boy's eye. Turning, he found it in the brooding west: a crooked finger of red lightning exiting the bellies of the clouds and disappearing into the horizon. He thought he heard voices too, distant voices rising in high screams, though it might have been his imagination and the whipping wind and crackling fires playing tricks on him.

Something else held the boy's attention there, though he was uncertain what it was. He watched the brewing sky guardedly, unease creeping the length of his spine like a stealthy serpent.

A moment later he turned at the iron touch on his shoulder. The old man's stormy eyes were examining him closely. He felt shaken, as if his thoughts were betrayed by his own tell-tale eyes. His mother's voice was in his thoughts then, gentle, soothing, like the sun in the sky of the before-days: *My darling, remember and always remember it: we can see a person—truly, deeply see and know them—through the windows of their eyes. This is how I first knew your father, and the good man he was.*

How he missed his parents, gone five years already. But he was grateful for the old man, who had taken him in when his home had fallen in the first great fire-rain and he'd had nowhere to go. The downtown neighbourhood in which their family lived had been decimated by the fires—the few survivors grew sick and were dead within days. Black boils grew on their bodies, leaking oily puss and filling their final days with agony until they grew too shrivelled with weakness to go on. They died, stinking and festering with bloody boils, like shrunken effigies of the people they'd once been. His parents had been among the fortunate: they'd burned alive amid the ruins of their house.

The boy had managed to escape, leaping from a bedroom window to run and duck amid the fire raining down. Somehow, he survived the plague that lingered afterward, to wander the wastes, eating any vermin he was quick enough to catch, once the supermarkets had been ransacked: mice and rats, and occasionally the delicacy of rabbit until their numbers dwindled and disappeared. And then he'd seen the old man silhouetted on the crooked horizon of an empty lot; the old man who walked deceptively like a rickety scarecrow but whose wiry arms had the strength to fight the fires like no man the boy had ever seen, even those much, much younger in years. Of course he'd joined the old man, and taken great satisfaction in aiding his efforts as he could, learning the ways of survival in the new wasteland, and the dangerous techniques of hunting the killing fires before they could burn him to a blackened husk the way his family had been killed.

"I'm sorry, sir," he muttered, shaken by the man's inquisitive observation. He hefted his pick to show that he was prepared to renew digging, but sensed the man's unwavering examination. He turned to him, cowering a little, the pick in his weary grasp trembling on the air.

"Boy," the man said in his voice of gravel, though the boy heard the way he sought to soften its rough edge, "What's got its hold on you?"

"Nothing, sir," the boy said. "I…I was only resting my arms."

The old man watched him a moment longer, then grunted and walked on. The boy followed, relieved. They stopped and peered up at the next fire-orb in their vicinity. This one hung too far over their heads to be dealt with properly, even with the extended reach of the wooden spears, so the man continued on down the litter-strewn street to the next. He walked to a place a little ways before it and, aiming carefully, plunged his spear into its underbelly. A screeching pierced the air, and a violent hissing as the vile life that pulsed within the orb seeped its way out and onto the wind. The flame sputtered and shook, and, uttering a final dying wheeze, the orb drifted down to earth, its flames diminished though not extinguished entirely. The man smashed his shovel's face down hard upon the thing several times until it was extinguished, grimacing at the pitiful weeping issuing from it.

The land around their house was rife with hanging fires. Try as he might, the man wasn't able to extinguish them all and soon enough many of them would have risen too high for him to be able to do anything about, and then he and the boy would have to leave the downtown core in which he'd lived for so many years. They would go southwards, to the county, though he'd heard that it was the same there. The fire-orbs had razed the farming communities and small towns, too, leaving the once-fertile land dead and un-tillable, families homeless and dying.

The old man hefted the smoking sac on the head of his shovel and walked carefully to a fire-hole located several feet away. The concrete around it was webbed with thick cracks, and he tested the ground with his foot before cautiously stepping to the ragged, charred edge of the hole itself. Peering down into its black mouth he felt relief, for the passage was clear of fallen rock debris. Carefully he extended the shovel down into the hole, slowly turned it in his hands, and let the orb-husk slide off its steel head and plunge into the darkness from which it had come.

He stepped quickly away from the hole, walking gingerly along the uncertain ground. Once beside the boy, he looked for the next orb in their vicinity and, finding it smouldering just beyond a row of abandoned cars, said, "There. Let's go." And off they went, the man leading, the boy scurrying to keep up. The air grew thicker with heat, and the distance was blurred with haze: it was always like this in areas rife with fire-orbs.

The Plague of Fires, as it had become known, had begun five years before: the flaming orbs appearing in the air everywhere, having burned through the ground and risen like sinister suns to mark the sky everywhere. The worldwide phenomenon of their five-year reign was one of utter devastation: fouling the land over which they shone, blighting crops and murdering forests and bringing sickness to those living near them. The symptoms of this illness bore a striking similarity to the bubonic plague of a century earlier: intense fevers; vomiting; excruciating body-wide pain; the formation of hard, black, pus- and blood-filled lesions; and death.

When risen to approximately twenty metres the orbs burst, raining down a ravenous fire that razed flesh, vegetation, and buildings like acid. Scientists around the world had been studying the singularity since it began and, though they'd gleaned a basic understanding of the mechanics by which the orbs functioned, had not come any closer to deciphering their true purpose nor what chemical agent made their fires so deadly. The most startling discovery was that the orbs were, in fact, living organisms, a species neither seen in any derivation throughout recorded history, nor even as part of cryptozoology's colourful catalogue of curiosities. Early theories that the orbs represented some new form of terrorist weapon were soon abandoned, owing to their global manifestation and to the fact that they were living creatures. Some saw them as Biblical and believed they represented a curse risen from Hell to lay waste to a world in dire need of paying penance for a long history of misdeeds.

The lifespan of an undisturbed orb, measured from when it first burst through the ground and reached its highest point of orbit, ranged widely, lasting from anywhere between four weeks to four years before it underwent its final natural combustion. In death the orbs proved the most deadly: like bombs, they erupted into immense balls of flame and plummeted to earth, resulting in catastrophic explosions as well as the mass release of their toxic properties into the atmosphere.

Their method of locomotion and their ability to hover had not been determined. Only their most basic life-patterns remained clear: that as they rose higher they likewise grew in size, and if allowed to maintain their orbits they grew substantially until, at some point, they combusted; when destroyed while closer to the ground they posed a lesser danger, because they hadn't yet achieved their adult size and so didn't contain as high a concentration of the fire and toxic agent that caused such destruction and sickness in those exposed.

Various methods of exterminating the fires had arisen over the years—the most effective means was shooting them down before they rose too high and grew very large, though any method of piercing their skin achieved the same end. The old man relied on ranging the land and hunting the things with spears he'd fashioned from the remaining trees in the area—his caveman method, he called it—for the simple reason that he'd long ago run out of bullets for his rifle, and with the surrounding shops long since ransacked for their provisions, he had no other place to turn.

Once punctured, the orbs died, though it was soon learned that the corpses needed to be disposed of quickly and efficiently because not long after death they underwent the same combustion as in their natural death cycle: the things would erupt into flame, resulting in the same devastation and disease to anyone in close proximity. Burying the things, whether in the tunnels from which they originally burst, or into new graves, was the only way to ensure that their final death-act would remain relatively harmless; though the prevalence of fire-sickness among humans in even those areas completely cleared of orbs attested to the strength of the things' toxins penetrating their earthen graves.

The fires had effectively devastated the world.

The old man drove the pick into the earth and, leaning on it, said, "I think I know you well enough now, boy, to tell when something is hounding you. Tell me: what troubles trouble you on this bitter day?"

The boy recalled this same appraisal from the old man only that morning over their breakfast of porridge, and again during their lunch of bread and soup warmed over the small fire in the street; even the night before, while standing in the doorway of the boy's bedroom, and watching him curled inside of his bed, when he'd lingered a moment longer than was customary. Now, though, in the openness of the wind-lashed street, the boy knew there was no escaping his guardian's concern.

"I asked you something, boy. You've been quiet and distant for days now." His eyes were intense but held a certain warmth. The boy saw this warmth, on occasion. Sometimes when the old man was at rest by the fireplace following a long day of orb-hunting among the ruins, drowsy in his cups, his heavy shoulders slumped inside of his hard wooden chair, when there was nothing that made it necessary for him to remain strong: on these rare occasions the boy found the warmth in the man's eyes.

"Sir," said the boy. "I've been thinking. The past weeks, I was… I want to know…I want to know about important things."

The old man frowned. "What things? What's this *important things*?"

The boy hesitated, flinching instinctively from the man's hand, which quivered at his side as if he wished to make a fist. He remembered that fist, for it had hit him and put stars in his vision on a few occasions, because the man was wont to become violent from time to time, when he was in his bottle or the fires in the world grew too quickly for him to contain and it put great fury in his heart. He stammered, "I mean…I mean *answers* to important questions, sir…"

The man's fingers became the fist the boy feared. "Don't you speak riddles at me, boy. Speak your mind or shut your mouth. You've been trying my patience for days now with your quiet mysterious ways."

"I mean…I was only wondering about things that…I want to know where it is…I want to know what there is…there." His eyes looked into the forbidding sky. "Past the clouds, and past the sky, and past the stars, and way out there." Here he gestured with both his hands, a sweeping gesture meant to encompass the entirety of the sky's mantle wheeling over them, and the world beyond the city. He ventured, "The city's a ghost town. No one lives here anymore, and maybe it's…different far away. And why are we…how do *we* survive, when so many others become sick and die…"

The man said, "We're stuck here, boy, on this dirty rock of fire and other curses—don't trouble yourself with questions that can never be answered. If you need reminding of our predicament, try turning on the radio or T.V. Or try finding the latest edition of a newspaper out here." He swept a hand toward the rubble towering all around them, all that remained of the city they'd once known. The wind keened among the empty houses, the only voice besides theirs in the quiet streets.

But the boy, disheartened as he was at being reminded of the dead radio and television set, felt bold. He'd been brave enough to finally broach the subject with the man and knew he had to go on. "But sir, this is what's been on my mind. I want…I need to try and learn the answers."

The old man's eyes brewed. When he spoke, his voice was hushed with an emotion the boy eventually understood was fear. "Is this important to you? Is this something you'll forget come tomorrow, or tomorrow after that? Or is this a real and true trouble to your heart?"

The boy, sensing the gravity of an imminent revelation, felt his heart begin a quickened hammering. "It's important, sir."

The man looked from the boy to the brooding west and to the boy again and then once more into the west before he said, "Bring your tools, boy. And pack your courage. Bring your faith, too. Bring it brimming in your heart."

In the wake of the words, he watched the child with a strangely tender gaze.

The boy felt the serpentine chill returning to creep along his spine.

"Come, boy."

The man walked across the street, away from the direction of the small house they shared in what had long ago been the western edge of the city's downtown core. He strode due west, where the sky brewed darkest with clouds.

Within minutes they arrived at the collapsed viaduct, its concrete sides scorched black. Its blackened remnants littered the gulley beneath street level, where a light mist hung. Down the garbage-strewn slope and into the gulley the old man wended his way, the boy scampering behind. They followed an ancient railroad track that cut through the weeds. In the distance, a small copse of black oaks had managed to avoid annihilation from the fires. Their leaves had long ago withered and died, and their trunks showed advanced signs of disease—their bark was mottled and strange, a deep green-black fungus crawling across the boles, though the skeletal husks stood tall and forbidding. As they neared the trees the boy felt it: their purpose lay there, among those withered trunks.

The wind grew violent, buffeting them. To the north, their American neighbour, Detroit, lay hidden behind a dense fog, though patches of the grey smouldered a deep red where orbs hung in profusion. Crimson flashes recurred in the fog-depths: lightning reaching down from the clouds toward the city.

The man stopped before they passed among the trees. His voice was cold as the day.

"I'm taking you to a foul place, boy. Maybe there's a lesson in the thing you'll see there. It's been there for many years. Here, in this black place, since long before you were born, boy. Each season that passes, when the sky pisses or snows, when the heat's enough to murder the strongest man, when the cold's bitter and deadly—it's always here, through it all. A sign, of what happened, of what might happen still."

The boy shivered in the wind or at the old man's enigmatic words. He didn't quite understand what he meant but feared the dark and mysterious quality of what he'd said, like a fairy tale with some grim lesson to be learned. He knew the dark endings of such tales.

The man went on stonily.

"It gibbers and it jabbers, and sometimes it sings in an angel's voice. It hollers with pain but mostly it speaks with a fury I've never heard so strong in any man. I…I don't know what it is, boy. I've heard men try to give it a name, but none knew for sure what they were seeing. Some believed it to have come from dark places. Like a description from Bible pages. I used to see it as one thing, and it gave me hope, but over the years—and it's been many years—it's become another thing. Maybe it's a reflection of the way things have turned out for us, today. I don't know. All I know is this thing… it's a *dangerous* thing. It's a dangerous thing to see, and to let into your heart. I know, boy. I know it well."

The boy looked to the trees, but they blocked whatever lay on the other side. His eyes were big and frightened.

The man said, "There have been men—long ago, and none of them are alive anymore as far as I know—who swore that the thing has the answers you're wanting to know, boy, if you've got the ears for hearing them. Few people own those ears. Come on."

And the old man took the boy's hand in his and led them through the trees and into the small natural clearing beyond.

When they were standing on the other side, the old man, eyeing the blackened husk straining at its bonds, said, "There it is, boy."

The boy stared, incredulous. His heart hammered. His blood grew cold.

"But, sir, she's just a…she's just a kid."

The man cocked an eye at the boy. "That's what you see, boy? A child chained there?"

The boy nodded vigorously. "Who put her here?" he said. "Who *chained* her up?"

"I don't know. No one knows. Maybe no one is supposed to know."

The girl parted the long tangle of her hair, and the boy saw her face clearly.

"Sir, she looks so much… She looks…Oh Jesus, sir…How could you have done this to her? It's my *sister*, sir. Oh, poor Jessica. It's *Jessica*."

The boy put a foot forward. The man stopped him with a hand on his bony shoulder.

"No," he said. "It tries to trick us. All men see what they want to see here, and so no man knows its true face. Your sister died in the first fires. You told me so yourself, boy."

"But sir," the boy protested, tears rising in his eyes. "She's here. *Here*. She's crying. She's cold. She's *blue* from the cold, sir. We have to—we need to help her."

But only the same word like a boulder dropping from the old man's mouth: "No."

The boy looked from his guardian to his sister weeping in her shackles. The bonds, he saw, bit into her thin wrists. Their rust had begun to infect her flesh, too: her wan skin was mottled with patches of black and sickly yellow. Her skin was a pale blue, a dead-looking colour. Tears rivered from her big emerald eyes and cut gnarled fingers down her filthy cheeks.

"But sir," squeaked the boy, feeling mouse-like and weak.

"Boy," came the man's voice from behind him. "Our time here is finished. If you've heard no answer to the riddle you want answered, then no answer is coming. You haven't the ears for it. But there's no shame in it. Come. Home waits for us. We can come back another time, and maybe what we see will be different then."

The boy scuttled forward, hands outstretched to free his sister from her agony. The man was quicker but only just. His burly hands landed on the child's scrawny shoulders. He flung the boy about. His open-handed blow across the child's cheek made a flat smacking sound. It stung. It drew pain but anger, too. The boy spat at the man who would abandon his sister, chained and naked and cold in the wilderness. He turned back to her again. The man lunged for the boy, caught him about his narrow chicken's legs. Together they tumbled to the raw rocky ground, wrestling in the dead grass. It was a moment's work for the man to pin the boy beneath him. Still the child fought. He spat at the man again. He cursed him, named him filthy things. The man smote him again, one open-handed blow of his palm across the boy's other cheek. The child scratched the man's hands and arms, drawing bloody lines. Again the man punched the boy, close-fisted now, knuckles connecting with his small cleft chin.

Watching their conflict, the chained girl called to them. The man heard its guttural croaking:

"They burn, old man. Your family roasts, you weakling. They each swallow the burning beastly cock of the Master forever. They choke to death on it even now while His hordes take turns raping their holes."

He sought to ignore its words but they cut deeply. He sought to reject the vision he'd glimpsed of it, jabbering with its mouthful of faeces and flies, masturbating with its legs spread wide and pelvis thrust toward him and the boy he'd been taking care of for the past five years, and who it was succeeding in turning against him during this, his first encounter with it.

The boy only fought the man harder at the plaintive sound of his sister's voice:

"Adam, I need your help. It hurts so *much*, Adam."

The boy wailed. Feeling pity for the mewling child, the man leaned close to whisper in the boy's ears: "Boy, *please*, be still. Home. We have to go home now. There are no answers for you here. We'll come back tomorrow and maybe what you see won't be what you see today. It's the way of this place, and of her. Right now, though, here there is only—"

The boy, pulling a large stone from the earth, brought its jagged face crashing upon the old man's temple. The man sagged back, stunned. Blood flowed freely from his head. The boy, seeing his chance at freedom, scrambled from beneath the man, momentarily extricating himself from his great weight. Still the man's vein-bulging hands reached for him, snagging his clothes. The boy snatched the shovel he'd dropped and swung. Its rusty edge landed on the man's head, felling him like a tree to the rocks.

He stared through befuddled eyes at the unmoving man. He watched blood pooling about his head. He heard her voice beseeching him:

"Oh, help me, brother. Oh, free me, *please*."

The boy went to her. He reached a hand to her shuddering little hand. He didn't notice the sound behind him—wouldn't have even guessed that the old man had found some superhuman-like reserve of strength to pick himself up from the ground after having his skull nearly split to the bone. And so he was saved by the hard two-handed blow the old man smashed across the back of his head.

The final vision the boy saw before blackness swallowed him was the creature whose hand was clutching his fingers: no longer his sister at all, no, but a dark thing; black-eyed; blood-mouthed; her hand wreathed in a ball of angry fire that burned his fingers even as consciousness abandoned him like all the hope he'd once had.

*

Though the old man had saved the boy from the thing in the field, carrying him back to their home in shaking arms, still a darkness came to hang over them both.

The boy grew sick in the days ahead. A dark and angry rash, mottled red and black, festered on the hand that had been held by the thing in the grove and crawled up his arm and his neck and all across the rest of his frail body. Food sickened him and he ate nothing. Skeletal and weak, he lay bedridden for weeks. Nightmares plagued him, and his delirious din kept the old man wakeful and watchful and with fingers clutching his silver cross through the deep dark mornings. He blamed himself, for giving in to the boy's troubled thoughts, and showing him the thing that he'd long suspected held some kind of answer to the great riddle of their times, the changing thing that sometimes deceived with hopeful visions, only to assassinate those hopes with their twisted reflection.

Perhaps he'd hoped the boy would do better than he had, and solve the riddle of the thing; glean some meaning from its treacherous words. But no. He'd only succeeded in getting the boy hurt, and shaking the foundation of the bond the two of them had shared for five long and difficult years.

The old man never left the boy's bedside. He tried feeding him soup and porridge and bread and, little by little, the child's appetite returned and, with it, his strength. His dreams came less frequently, and less darkly, and after about a month he was able to sleep the whole night through untroubled. Weeks after this he was able to leave the bed on his own, walking without help from the old man, so that he could relieve and wash himself.

One morning, while taking their breakfast on the rotting wooden porch, the man caught the boy staring off across the cracked and charred street to the west, where the dark copse of trees blighted the gully. The man ventured, "It's a loneliness, boy, isn't it? Once you understand…once your heart understands the truth in it. There's nothing coming for us, boy, but more days like this one, and then darkness. And the hope it gives you—any hope at all—it calls to you. It *pulls* at you."

"I don't…I can't believe that there's nothing good coming for us, sir."

The man turned to him, impressed. He said, "Boy, you've become a man. You've been through a great darkness and come through to the other side, changed, and stronger. Your choices are yours, and no one else's." And standing he said, "Come on. Up with you. A man must learn to walk on his own, even when walking is difficult and dangers abound. And we have a lot of work to do yet, after you've come back."

He gestured out across the ruins, punctuated with the fire-plumes everywhere.

"Hell is rising up everywhere, boy," he said, eyes grim. "Our job will never be done here, but that doesn't mean we do our job without reason."

The boy, now a man, left the rickety porch and walked with bold steps westward. He crossed the broken street, past rusted hulks of cars stilled forever, past brittle blackened skeletons swimming in clothing rotted to tatters that clung like webs among the bones; he descended into the fog-filled gully and found the rusty train track and followed it into the mist; and he pushed his way resolutely through the ring of diseased black oaks, where stunted branches snagged him and evil little shrubs clawed at his hair and clothes. He came into the grove of blasted, fire-eaten land.

She was there, and beckoned him with her large jewel eyes and small whimpering mouth.

"Adam, you've come to free me."

He said, "I've come to talk with you. I have questions. Maybe you have the answers."

II: Yesterday the Fire-Breathers

He couldn't recall a specific point at which his relationship with everything in his world had fractured. It seemed that a long and gradual decline must have taken place over the years, or else maybe everything had always been like this and he'd only recently come to see it for what it was. He considered the people he'd called his friends and whom he hadn't seen nor spoken with in so very long. He tried to conjure their faces but found with some despair that only portions of their features came to him, and these only imprecisely, as if he were seeing them through dirty glass.

Wandering the streets he found himself hating everything. The people he passed on the sidewalks: he loathed them. The ramshackle houses and old tenements: they filled him with despair, too, though significantly less than the people, with their manically drugged eyes or expressions as lost-looking as he felt himself; or just their brief glances of indifference before turning back to the cell phone in their hands or inward to whatever conversation they were having with themselves. This was the downtown core he knew too well, the streets he'd grown up in and which he now, as an adult who felt much older than he was, still found himself wandering as aimlessly as in the years before.

He was passing the liquor store, resisting the pull of the place's automated doors sliding open in temptation as the sensor detected his presence on the sidewalk—when he was stopped by a little elderly man. The man stood off along the building's wall, and when he'd got his attention with a small wave of his gloved hand he stepped out onto the sidewalk. He had a shambling limp that combined with his squat stature to make him appear leprechaun-like and a little unnerving. He looked lost inside the giant parka he wore, flowing and toga-like. His eyes, peering out from beneath a ratty toque, glimmered with a vitality that seemed wholly incongruous with his shabby clothing. He spoke, but because his mouth was hidden behind his enormous scraggly beard and moustache, the sound seemed oddly disconnected from him. His voice was gentle though, at odds with his haggard, pock-marked face illuminated beneath the orange light of the streetlamps.

"It's a cold, cold night." And with the words he took a step back to once more lean against the rough stucco of the liquor store building.

The old man seemed to be waiting expectantly, which struck him as odd. He felt that his statement demanded a deeper appreciation and response but didn't know what to say, so only agreed on the frigid temperature. "Yeah. It's freezing. The wind off the river is bad tonight."

The leprechaun-man said, "It's much colder than that, friend. When you think about it."

He stepped aside for a couple leaving the liquor store, so that he found himself standing flush along the building's wall beside the little old man. This gesture, he felt, signified some type of social line being crossed: where before he'd been his own solitary man wandering the night streets, he now was a member of whichever tribe this little old man belonged to. Standing there side by side, they were sharing something, a camaraderie or kinship or something deeper than this, that any of the pedestrian passers-by or drivers idling at the intersection would clearly see.

And in the silence they shared, the old man's words returned to him. Suddenly he understood. It was much colder tonight than merely a wind off the water that bit you deep could account for; it was colder than any barometer would tell you. It went deeper than this, beyond easy documentation or classification or description of any kind.

It was a cold *world*.

With some astonishment, he felt able to tell the little man things he'd never spoken of to anyone else before, though he knew not why. And, his initial unease evaporated, he said, "I left my wife. A little over one month ago."

The diminutive old man nodded. There was compassion in his eyes, and something else that looked to the man like worry. He ventured, "Why? Why did you leave her, son? If you don't mind my asking?"

He considered this. He admitted, "It's complicated. These things always are, right? I don't know. I really don't know why I left her, except… All I know is that I looked at her, and I saw her in a way I'd never seen her before. In a way I never thought I would see her. Suddenly she made me unhappy—" He stopped short, shaking his head. "No," he corrected himself. "No, that's wrong. What I mean is that I looked at her, very closely, and I remembered so many things in the looking, you see? Our years together. Before marriage, and after. I looked into her eyes and I saw all of these things. And then I realized she no longer gave me the happiness she once did. And I knew I no longer gave her any joy, either. And then I thought of the world, and knew that there was no more goodness left in it either. And just like that, I left her. In bed. Crying. I explained myself as much as I was able to put it into words, but I probably did a poor job of it. I tried, though. And I left her there. I've been walking ever since. Here I am."

The little old man eyed him with inscrutable eyes. He said nothing. The wind whipped against them.

"Is there… Have you found your happiness again, out here?" The old man gestured with a gloved hand into the street unfurling westwards. The light from its streetlamps and scattered shop fronts wavered in the misting rain.

The man shook his head. "There's no more happiness. Not for me. Wherever I go, it's always gone." He smiled as he said it, because in the saying he felt free of some small part of the burden of carrying the knowledge. He'd never thought he could share this with anyone, let alone a stranger.

The little old man watched him evenly, his eyes betraying some deeper, unspoken knowledge or wisdom. He said, "There's a coffee shop close by. Let me buy you a drink. I want to tell you a story, but it's too violent out here." The rain was falling harder now, making a staccato pattering on the cement, and he pulled his hood down lower around his bearded face.

"You'll buy me a drink? Excuse me for saying, but I thought you might be… homeless. You're not?"

The old man's wrinkled face creased even more as he smiled wryly beneath his bushy beard. Under his thick white eyebrows his eyes were grave. "No. I only look that way. And sometimes feel that way too. But in the traditional sense of the word, no, I ain't homeless. I've got a roof over my head. Now come on, friend."

He felt compelled to offer the old man an apology but the wind rose and whipped at them in a renewed frenzy and continuing their conversation out on the sidewalk felt suddenly an achievement beyond his strength. He huddled into himself, breathing into his wool scarf and pushing his gloved hands deep into the pockets of his coat.

The old man said no more either, only turned and shuffled westward along the sidewalk. After a moment he followed him. The wind and rain buffeted them as they went, as if seeking to repel their progress in the most urgent way.

*

The coffee shop was pre-dawn sleepy: a pair of weary-looking employees loitered behind the counter talking in low voices, a teenaged girl with acne on her cheeks and her supervisor, a middle-aged woman with a haggard face and throaty smoker's voice and small cautious eyes, as though they'd seen their share of deceptions and were now conditioned to watch everyone and everything she encountered with the utmost suspicion. There were no patrons but themselves, huddled over their paper cups in one corner of the quiet room, the murmuring television set mounted on the wall showing a re-airing of the previous evening's news broadcast.

The coffee shop was located in the sparsely populated periphery of the downtown core, tucked away on a side street of derelict buildings and boarded-up shop fronts off the hive of busier streets that ran south of the river. At this time of the morning, the sidewalks in this section were frequented only by prostitutes and homeless and the occasional person looking to sober up with a quick coffee before heading home following a night of dedicated drinking.

"Thanks for the coffee," said the man, holding the cup between his hands. "I need it to warm up."

"It's nothing," said the old man.

Looking at him now, the man saw that the leprechaun-man appeared less old than he'd initially believed. His eyes were still animated, though their grim character remained.

"You were going to tell me a story," said the man to the old man.

The old man nodded, seeming revivified by their early morning conference. "Oh, I've got a story for you, friend. This is what done put me out into the fog and rain this morning, like you. Listen:"

He forgot the paper cup in his fingers, though it scalded his skin. He would listen intently, for the story's message, for its significance in relation to him, which he somehow understood would be contained within the tale.

The old man tapped his fingers across a newspaper that had been left by a previous patron and rested on the table between them. "I don't need to open the pages here to know the stories they tell. They're the same stories every day. Every serial killer uncaught. Every victim winked out of existence in the world. Every bomb dropped and bullet fired and war fought. Every secret crime committed on every man and woman and child. All of these things are getting worse, more common in the days, and, taken together, they form a *sign*. They signal where we are today. There have always been signs for those with the eyes to see them, but now the auguries come daily. Only last night I read in the newspaper that strange fires were seen in the county, rising from the ground and into the sky. Thousands witnessed the phenomenon. Scientists, they seek to study it, priests to pray against it. Some say that the end is coming, my friend, and quickly. They're wrong. The end came a long time ago. We're living in the end times today. We have been for some time. But despite this, and the great sadness it puts into your heart like it puts it into mine, despite this, I can show you joy again."

He watched the raggedy old man avidly. Any skepticism he might have had left him in the wake of the dark soliloquy. He no longer trembled from his time outdoors in the terrible wind. The coffee, the doughnut shop, the man's words: something had warmed him, thawed the cold that had crept into his bones. The old man's eyes as he talked grew wilder. For the first time the man noticed their bright blue colour: he'd once been a handsome man, this time- and memory-ravaged man.

"I could tell the moment I seen you walking down the sidewalk tonight," he said to the man studying him, hanging on his every word. "I seen the look in your eyes, and it's the look I see whenever I look in the mirror during these strange, hungry days we're in. So I'm making you an offer. If you want to see it, friend, there's a chance I can show you your joy again, so the next time you look in the mirror you'll see it too, a little bit of the joy you used to know, before you grew up and started to know the way of the world. And maybe once you have it back it'll make living in it easier to bear."

This was the umpteenth time the old man had called him *friend*. Nobody else had called him *friend* in a very long time. He found tears in his eyes hearing it from the man now, for the word carried sincerity and this show of kindness was overwhelming after his self-imposed exile from the life he'd known. He found himself nodding in earnest agreement and, following the old man's example, he stood from the table and donned his coat and toque and gloves.

They crossed to the door.

They stepped from the coffee shop and into the funereal morning: the light of near-dawn blighted by the overcast sky and the dense fog billowing through the streets. A heavy silence hung everywhere, broken occasionally by a cautious car navigating through the mists, its headlights fighting for visibility.

The old man led them out onto the sidewalk and they began an unhurried pace westward. They didn't speak, hunkering down and burying their faces in their scarves in an effort to stave off the chill air. Several minutes later they found themselves approaching the viaduct that rose high to overlook a gulley striped with multiple rows of rusty train tracks cutting through the wild grass.

Something caught the man's eye, some bright movement among the fog and murky greenery. He squinted, following the movement. Smiling, he said, "A fox! There's a fox down there."

The old man nodded. "Oh yes. He's always down there. And the others too."

The man looked again into the gulley. Sure enough, he saw them there: a racoon meandering along the base of the gulley where the grass rose steeply to the street above, nosing about in the weeds; and close to it, a tawny cat peering up at them curiously; and beyond the cat, a mangy mutt, its rain-wet coat glistening in the orange light thrown down from the street lamps, sitting directly beside another fox, this one much smaller, a cub perhaps.

"That's amazing," the man said. "They're all together. I've never seen that before."

The old man was nodding again. "No, my friend, you haven't. But here you'll see it often. It's where the pure of heart gather, I think." And he turned and began a cautious limping descent along the wet grassy slope toward the gulley below.

"Where are we going?" The man was watching the old man shuffle down with wary eyes. This all seemed so strange, and unreal.

The old man's voice carried from below, softly, "Come on. This is the way."

The man hurried after him, nearly slipping and plunging down the steep incline several times. He arrived at the bottom a moment after the old man and stood surveying the gulley from his new vantage: the ravine's floor stretched on toward the river, mist-shrouded, dense with bushes and trees lining either side. The animals were unperturbed by their presence, intensifying the dream-like feeling permeating the scene: the adult fox watched him a moment with curious eyes before returning its attention to foraging in the grass; the raccoon did the same; and the dog, cat, and fox cub seemed more interested in keeping their vigils watching the fog-shrouded gulley than these two humans trespassing in its green depths.

The old man set off again without further word. He hurried to walk abreast of him. As they trudged along, parallel to the tracks, the old man spoke softly, another unsettling monologue like some street poem of the apocalypse.

"I don't know what it means, friend, but I've seen it here for years. And though it's the key to the joy I been telling you about, it frightens me good, too. Good and deep. A fear into my bones. Sometimes it's all I feel out here, in the streets and fields. This fear, knowing I'm alive in the same world as…this. Because… Because, you see, every place has one. I've tried living in different places, but it's done me no good trying to look away. I was born here, but made my way across the province, to Hamilton to London to Toronto, further along to Forest and Tobermory, even into Detroit across the river, for a time. And then back here, because it's where I began and I guess I figured it might as well be the place I finish, too. And I can vouch for the truth of it: they're in every city and town man built on this Earth. This is something I know. I've seen with my own eyes, and feel it in my heart. I *know*."

The old man stopped walking, watching his companion with an intense tragedy in his eyes, before plunging into the dense wall of foliage growing alongside the tracks. The man followed, parting overhanging branches and stepping gingerly among the great tree roots that emerged from the soil like the knuckles of giants' fingers. They passed through a colony of pale white flowers, brilliant as snow in the gloomy gulfs of the trees, before the branches closed closer together, and brambles rose everywhere like natural barbed wire. They wended their way carefully, slowly, the thorny branches snagging in their coats. A sound, or sounds, drifted to the man through the foliage. He whispered, "I heard something. An animal?"

The old man's whisper came back to him: "Animals come here, yes. Big and small. I've seen families of deer. Hawks and owls watching from the trees." He was slipping onward again, merging into the foliage ahead. The man hurried to keep pace with him through the thick gloom. They whispered silently through the bushes, the fog much denser here in the gulley bottom than in the streets above.

The old man stopped and turned to his companion. His voice was quiet, his eyes solemn.

"We're here." He watched the man a moment longer, before nodding and turning to part the brambles that clung like fungus along a chain-link fence that ran on into the woods in both directions as far as the eye could see. A large ragged hole was cut through the wire. Stooping, he stepped through carefully, and the man followed, un-snagging his coat from the rusted edges of the clipped mesh. He came up beside the little old man and found that they were in a glade ringed by black oaks, the treetops to the east overseen by the black glassless windows of the abandoned hospital like countless blind eyes. Together they looked upon the site of scalded earth. The breath hissed from between the man's clenched teeth, the exclamation loud in the stillness.

A great winged woman lay in a heap upon the scorched grass. She struggled against her shackles, a complex latticework of stout chains wound tightly about her naked body, entwining her waist, slung over her shoulders and across her breasts. Her wrists and ankles were manacled in huge rusty irons. Though the chains kept her limbs huddled inwards her Amazonian size was clear. The muscles of her arms and legs bulged as she strained against her bonds. Her broad shoulders threatened to snap the fetters against which they fought.

She'd managed to squeeze her immense wings, their skin the same moon-colour as the rest of her, through apertures in the tangle of her bonds. They beat violently, creating a strong wind that whipped the clothes against their bodies.

Her long silver hair was matted with mud and bits of foliage, her bare arms and legs and breasts were dirty, too. Though her long lithe figure radiated strength, her struggles were ineffectual against her bonds, her mighty wings lifting her from the ground only a few inches before she sagged earthwards time and again at the behest of the chains. Her face was partially hidden behind her filthy hair, though her eyes were visible: determined, furious, proud. And though they stood very near to where the winged woman struggled it seemed as though she didn't notice them at all, as if they watched her from a great distance or through some membranous wall beyond which she, inexplicably, couldn't quite see. Or perhaps she merely focused her energy on her struggle, and paid no attention to those gawking at her predicament.

The old man's voice was grave. "It'll be gone come dawn. Every morning it is. But every night—at dusk, without fail—it's here again."

"She's too beautiful. I can't… It's hard to look at her, for more than a moment at a time."

The un-homeless man nodded. His eyes were solemn, and he watched his companion closely.

"Should we try to—Are we supposed to help her?"

"*Her*, you say? No—she can't be helped, friend. She won't let you help her, even if we could.

I know. I know. I once tried myself. I offered her my hand and her great wings swept me away like a crumb until I was flat on the grass right on this very spot we're standing on now. No, she can't be helped, friend. This is her enslavement."

"By whom?" he asked. "Who enslaved her?"

The old man shuddered. "It seems to me this world beat her. Maybe it couldn't bear the beauty of her, and it chewed her up and chained her here as punishment for having found her visiting here. I can't be certain, friend, but my heart tells me it's so. This bitter, dying world is pulling all the beauty and miracles down into the fire with it."

The man couldn't stop staring at her. "She's so young. A child. Who could want to do this to her?"

"Is that what you see? A child?" The old man's tone was matter-of-fact. As though he'd heard this description of the vision before, as though he might not see it the same way.

"Who do you see?" the man said.

At this the old man's eyes grew strained, nostalgic, distant. "Sometimes my sister, dead twenty years. Sometimes I see a stranger. A woman I never saw before. Once I saw my father. Twice I saw my mother. When she was young. My mother before she was old and crooked and dying from the cancer that got her in the end. In the end, it's mostly the same: I see *goodness* chained there in that circle of dead grass and earth, though sometimes a dark thing struggles there, too, and that thing

I'm deeply afraid of. But mostly I see goodness. Mostly. And that I take as a gift. But right now, at this moment, I see something close to what you described. Something strong, something good like that."

A desperation tugged inside the man's chest. "Doesn't anyone… Does anyone else *know* about this?"

"Look, friend."

He followed the man's eyes, and started at the sight: a figure lurking among the shadowed foliage at the periphery of the tree-line that fringed the edge of the ravine on its west side, a man huddled inside of a large parka, eyes hidden beneath the fur-lined hood. Another figure a ways behind him, a portly woman, head covered in a checkered bandana, beheld the winged woman from her place seated on a large, smooth-sided white rock embedded in the mud just beyond the scraggly trees. Near to her was another man, wearing a grey suit beneath his navy windbreaker, watching the scene with troubled eyes. There were tears visible on his cheeks as he wept freely. Even more startling was the tall middle-aged man peering from behind a thin tree beyond him: his dark uniform camouflaging him in the gloom but the silhouette of his pistol and nightstick revealing him to be a police officer. At his foot, a plump possum sat hunched, staring into the glade, its tiny dark eyes shining.

The old man startled him when he took his hand in his own and held it tightly. He said, "It's in your eyes, friend. I noticed it the moment you came out of the fog like a ghost. It's the reason I talked to you, and brought you here. Lost eyes I see plenty. I own them, too. But *kind* eyes… Those are a rare sight, friend."

The man looked back to the winged woman. Still, she struggled against her chains, her movements causing the mist to swirl and eddy about her.

"What does it mean?"

"As far as I'm able to figure it, it means that, right now, this early morning, I'm here and you're here—and the others over there and there and there—and she's here, too." The old man nodded to the winged woman. "Isn't that enough? Isn't it enough, knowing that? And being brought together here, to see the beauty of her—the *will* and *determination* of her—in the middle of another dark night in this dark world?"

A pattering began in the leaves and trees around them: rain again, harder than earlier in the morning. The man looked to the sky. "My God, it looks like smoke, or ashes," he said, watching the ceiling of black clouds churning in the violent wind, reflections from orb-fires casting an evil light to pulse across the heavens like some monstrous aurora.

"I think it might be," said the old man. "That makes the most sense to me, too. This world's been burning from the very moment man crawled out of the muck and lifted the first stick that killed his first brother. It's been burning from the beginning, and still we haven't learned. But we're going to keep on living."

They turned back to watch the winged woman.

It took the man a while to understand what he was feeling. It crept subtly into him at first, and then he was very suddenly overwhelmed with the sensation: warmth; a comforting warmth. He looked wondrously to the old man beside him. "My God," he said, amazed, amazed at the smile he couldn't help from appearing on his face. "You were right. This...Seeing this, and being here, with everyone else...It's..." He drifted off, smiling still, not knowing how to express what he felt.

The old man finished for him. "Your faith—in whatever good things you once had faith in—has been renewed." He turned his jewelled eyes on him, and he smiled a toothless smile, all red inflamed gums and cold-cracked lips, but beautiful, too. "Mine has been renewed too. It is most times I visit here. We may feel weak in the face of the great storm, my friend, but at least we have each other. We can only hope it'll be enough, when whatever's coming our way is done with us. Because I can feel it in these old bones—something *is* coming, hot on the heels of everything that's come before."

Watching the old man, awash in gratitude, a realization came over him. "I don't even know your name. My name is Ray."

The old man smiled. "Nice to know you, Ray. I wish I could tell you what I was called but I don't even remember. It's been too long, and it doesn't matter much anyways. Call me *friend.* Call me *brother*. Those sound best to me."

Ray nodded, and turned back to the grove and the spectacle it held.

He and the old man—and the fat woman and the businessman and the police officer and the homeless woman, as well as the homeless man and grocery store clerk who arrived a few minutes later—they stood in the wind, unspeaking, watching the chained figure in the fading moonlight, perhaps each seeing it differently, knowing she would be gone soon, disappeared with the arrival of dawn but knowing she would return the following night. And they were grateful for the promise of her return, and the promise of her untiring struggle against the bonds chaining her in her place of scorched earth and darkness; and for the beating of their hearts, made to pound stronger and with more resolve, every moment passing while in her presence.

*

III: Tomorrow a New Age

The old man sat on a small heap of rubble before his home, like a king upon a throne carved from the fabric of the old world beneath his feet. He was waiting for the boy—new, changed, recognizable or not at all—to come forth from the wilderness following his expedition of discovery. Behind him rose the remains of buildings like a crooked row of decaying teeth, some brown-brick tenements blackened and melancholy, other structures merely ragged stumps with their tops long ago shorn away by the otherworldly kiss of the Fire Plague.

He scanned the crooked horizon, marked everywhere with the hanging fires, searched among the rubble of the distant viaduct. His eye caught movement, a figure clambering among the debris. He watched it avidly, wondering at its uncanny gait over the uneven earth; too smooth, its movement, as if it travelled over soft grasses rather than the shattered bedrock like a devastated No Man's Land.

Perhaps the old man's eyes played tricks, or else the landscape and the day's weird light worked together to conjure a mirage. It looked as if the boy was drifting through the air, bare feet hanging inches over the scarred earth. Majestic, full of beauty like creatures of religion and lore he remembered having read stories of, long ago.

He closed his eyes. As he waited he wondered whether this dream he dreamed was a dream after all. The old man stood from his rock. He straightened his shoulders and opened his eyes and his eyes hardened. He was prepared to face whatever kind of man the boy had become following his trial in the world.

The young man drew close. His face was radiant. His eyes clear. His voice friendly.

"Hello there. I…I'm not sure…Something happened but I can't remember what exactly. But…But I know I want…I *need* to find others—other people, like yourself. I will find them all, and show them…love. Together, we'll be stronger than alone."

"That's a good plan," the man said. "Someday the fires will be put out for good, and the world remade. Someday the green trees will abound. Someday there will be Eden again."

He felt his faith alive inside himself like a heartbeat. He believed in it. He trusted in it. He cherished and loved it. He had to, for if he didn't his soul would be lost. The first reports had begun trickling in days before from survivors he'd crossed paths with on his fire-hunting forays into the city, and only that morning the man had seen them for the first time himself.

The old man peered upward. The young man followed where he looked and together they saw:

The array of lights high in the sky to the east, shimmering like stars but much, much closer: different from the fire-orbs that had risen from below to char the earth, these lights were frosty and blue—and they were descending from the heavens above, heading toward an inevitable collision with the fire-orbs infesting the sky everywhere.

"What does it mean?"

The old man smiled at the young man. "We'll see. Let's watch together, and we'll see."

The young man, turning to look at the old man, said, "My name is…Adam?" He said it like a question. His brow wrinkled in thought, as if he were trying hard to remember, past some difficult thing blocking his memory. And then he offered the old man his hand. "Who are you?"

The old man smiled, a gesture equally melancholic and wonder-filled. His name: he hadn't had reason to think of or say his name aloud in so very long. Was he the same man he was before, when he'd had a name by which others had called him? His name—what had it been? What *was* it?

Like a sun-ray, you brighten even my darkest days:

The phrase came to him unexpectedly, the first poetry he'd ever heard, from a time so long ago it seemed unreal. Words from his mother.

Like a sun-ray.

Sun-ray.

Ray.

Ray!

He smiled at the memory.

Over the furious, omnipresent crackling of fire the old man made his voice strong.

"I don't remember my name anymore, and names don't matter in the end anyways. But you can call me *father*."

There is Only One

Into the bedroom darkness and silence:

"Are you awake still?"

"Of course."

"I...have a confession."

"I know. I've been waiting."

"I've...I've done a really terrible thing."

(*A glorious thing*)

"I know. I can...I've been able to tell, for a while now. Ever since you vanished…and came back."

"And for that…I'm sorry."

"I know."

"You have no idea how sorry. To you."

"Okay."

"I can't even begin to explain how sorry I am."

"Tell me."

"I'm so sorry."

"Tell me. You owe me that much."

"I'll tell you."

*

It was a day like any other day, or so it seemed when I crawled out of bed and crawled to work. Work was shit as usual. Warehouse work can't be anything else. My back was broken by noon, and lunch was over too soon and then nothing but more lifting and box-cutting and pushing skids until the end of day. If I never see another box again it'll be too soon.

Then I was out the door and headed home. I'd had the idea to grab some takeout for us, so I nipped into the burger joint on Wyandotte near Howard. I placed our order and went next door to the magazine shop while they made our food. I was looking through magazines— the new issue of Classic Pulps had come out—when...when she found me there.

I don't know what compelled me to do what I did. Her eyes maybe. Something in *them. Maybe the way she spoke to me. Her voice—it wasn't like a normal...it wasn't like any voice I'd heard. I can't even remember any particular quality it had, like if it was deep or high but only that she spoke like a song being sung. It was music. And I forgot about the magazine, and our food cooking next door. I forgot about you and I forgot about myself and I forgot about us. I forgot about the world and life and I followed her from the magazine shop. Literally, I followed her the whole way—she was always a few feet ahead of me. Sometimes she'd look back and her eyes would confirm why I was following her. Something in them that...*

spoke. Her eyes spoke even though, during that whole walk, she said nothing to me. We walked for a long time. I was peripherally aware of the fact that all the people I was passing on the street had no idea what was going on, that I was being led— being made to follow—this woman, almost against my will. Or, a better way to put it, they weren't aware that any willpower I'd had before had been…removed. Shut off.

We walked and walked. Thirty minutes, forty minutes. We came into the industrial district past the downtown core, past the doughnut shop and vacant storefronts. It was like a ghost town. No pedestrian traffic at all, a car here or there but not many. She led us through a hole in a tall chain-link fence, and down a grassy slope into the gully that runs underneath the old bridge with the train track running under it.

I followed her home. This was where she lived.

She had a nest—it's the only way I can describe it—a nest, under the overpass on University Avenue. Down there, in all the trees and grass and tangles. There's garbage there too. People throw stuff over the bridge, old furniture, bags, papers, whatever. In there, deep in all those trees and grass, she has her hole. It's an actual hole in the grass, in the side of the little rise leading down to the old train yard on the opposite side from where we'd come down into the gully. She went in and I followed her. It was a tight squeeze. We went in on our stomachs, crawling. I had to wriggle my body, pull myself inch by inch through the tunnel. I never questioned what I was doing. I had to do it. Inside it was warm. Really hot. Hot and clammy, like a greenhouse. The walls were just dirt, soil, packed tight. I saw worms in the walls, just poking out and travelling up and down the walls and ceiling.

I could see around me perfectly, and it looked like our skin was...it's like we glowed. Or like there was firelight flickering over our bodies, and across the walls of the nest, but there was none. I couldn't figure out where the light was coming from. Now I understand that it came from her.

At some point I looked at her and she was naked. She was perfect. So perfect it was almost hard to look at her directly. She was…too much. There was too much...beauty. That much beauty is…frightening. She had a...tail. She had a tail. *I...It drew me like... It compelled me. Like a spell. Like I was in a trance. Her tail was long and wet and it moved like a tongue. It lapped at the air. It was like a spell. The tail-tongue, her, the nest, everything. It was a spell and it had me.*

The ground was a grass carpet. Thick. She laid down there and I laid beside her. It was so soft, the grass. Softer than any grass I'd ever felt in my life.

We made love. And if I'm being honest, that's exactly what it was. Making love, not just sex. Not just fucking, which it would have been had it been any other person. Any other ordinary person. If it had been anyone else it wouldn't have happened at all. And it would never have been love.

When it was done we didn't talk. I couldn't move. I had no strength. I felt like I'd lived my entire life and was looking back on everything. And then, at some point, she showed me out. I didn't want to go but I obeyed her. I begged her to let me stay with her but I obeyed her. It was dawn outside. I couldn't believe it. I'd been in her nest all night and morning. And then when I got home I found out I'd been missing for six days. I hadn't eaten at all while I'd been in there, but I wasn't hungry or thirsty. I'd never felt better in my life. Stronger, and so healthy. Like I'd slept a million years and could stay awake for the rest of my years.

But the last I saw of her was...I can't even explain it because...It doesn't compute with...And yet it does, but...I heard her voice whispering in my ear after I'd crawled from her nest, and I looked and she was gone, but there, in the wild grass, was a giant snake. It was dark red and black. And huge. Like something from out of prehistory. It was watching me from the wildflowers, and then it slipped off and disappeared in the woods nearby.

I went back there. I've been back there every day since that night. I went back early this morning. But I couldn't find her nest. I can never find it. I swear I remember exactly where it was, but it's not there anymore. I looked for hours today. I covered every inch of the gulley, time and again, over and over and over. But there's nothing. She's gone. She's gone. *I felt so alone. I* feel *so alone. The loneliness gets stronger, so much worse, every day that goes by. Every minute passing feels like a thousand years. She's gone.*

She's still here, somewhere in the world. I know that. I feel her. But she's gone from my life, and all I can do is wonder where she is and if she'll ever find me again.

Suddenly there was light.

She'd turned on the bedside lamp. He blinked in its vicious glare and found her watching him evenly. Her eyes were hurt and scared, but mostly she looked furious, as if she might hit him. He was stunned to realize that he'd made his confession with complete honesty, leaving out no detail, not censoring his feelings about what happened. He knew in that moment that he was still held in the grip of the spell—that he would always be.

"Well, you enjoy your tailed monster women. There are plenty of those out there, you evil piece of psycho fucking shit."

No, there's only one.

But he didn't say the words. He gave her this final gift, and watched her get dressed and gather her belongings and leave the room and his life forever.

With her gone, his partner of five years—five good years, relative to the old world he'd known—he felt no different, though he truly was sorry for having hurt her. But he'd lost something infinitely more precious. His desolate heart pined for it.

Magic, and its promise that there was more to this life for him if only it found him again.

He waited a few minutes, long enough that it would be certain his once-girlfriend had had time enough to walk down the three flights of stairs, climb into her car and tear out of the apartment building's small parking lot.

Then he climbed from the bed, shirtless, and left the building. Once on the street, feeling the cooling cement through the soles of his bare feet, he turned and found the moon hanging overhead.

And he ran, into the night, feeling its embrace as he searched for the only thing in the world that could cure the emptiness and the death in his heart.

Gods and Devils and Those Caught Between

Janice, eagle-eyed, saw first. Eyes wide in astonishment and outrage, snarling, she pointed at something beyond the tangle of black oak branches and wild grass through which the two of them had been walking, hand in hand.

Tim jockeyed for a better vantage, straining to catch sight of something out of the or—

He saw: past the edge of the crab apple-dotted foliage, in the small glade beyond: movement. A flash of bright purple, the cotton of a t-shirt…

They inched closer, placing their sneakered feet delicately in the soft soil, avoiding small branches and early-fallen leaves strewn everywhere for fear of giving away their position.

They were nearly at the verge of the foliage-line, and could now see him perfectly. It was one of their classmates, Derek Combar. He was stomping feverishly on the ground, grunting in tandem with each footfall, appropriately caveman-like and savage (Derek was the most notorious and feared playground torturer at Forest Grove Public School). It was only as he walked in a tight circle around the place where he'd stomped that they saw the pile of grey fur, matted dark with blood. A raccoon, its body flattered by the blows rained down on it by the boy who'd ambushed it.

Both of them saw it when the animal spasmed, a convulsive movement of agony—it was still alive, and being slowly murdered by their classmate.

Janice and Tim didn't discuss it. They unsheathed the knives they liked to carry in the waistbands of their shorts whenever they adventured in the woods, pretending they were barbarians fighting demons, like the heroes of the pulp stories they liked to read together in the shade of the oaks, taking breaks to kiss and touch each other. They'd always known demons were real. Finally, they'd found one in the flesh, and finding it there doing its grisly work validated something else they'd long believed: Derek Combar, schoolyard tyrant, was the very Devil himself. To torture and murder an innocent and beautiful animal like the raccoon for no other reason than to feel its body and its skull break under his feet... *This* was *evil.* They saw his veil of artifice lifted at last, so well maintained in the school-day illusion they shared: the raw-meat skin, bleeding everywhere; the silver serpent writhing from his mouth, its sibilant voice haunting the gloom; the hexad of horns blooming from his forehead, the bone-crown decreeing him emperor of the twilight-world, and challenger to the sunlit kingdom above.

They held their knives low, ready for the one-two upper-thrusts they'd practised so many times in the gloomy places of those woods where sunlight filtered through only a little, a little.

Janice stopped Tim with a hand on his forearm. She mouthed it at his ear, less than a whisper but loud enough to fill his heart:

I love you.

He nodded, never taking his eyes from the Adversary.

Around them, the songs of bluejays mingled with the percussion of meaty blows.

The children crept closer, rogue sunbeams finding the naked blades in their fists, flashing like signals from watching gods above.

The Devil, at long last, was going to pay.

About the Author

Alexander Zelenyj is the author of the books *Blacker Against the Deep Dark*, *Songs for the Lost*, *Experiments at 3 Billion A.M.*, *Black Sunshine*, and others. A compendium of his work, *These Long Teeth of the Night: The Best Short Stories 1999-2019*, was published by Fourth Horseman Press. His newest book is the short story collection, *Beware Us Flowers of the Annihilator*.

Zelenyj lives in Windsor, Ontario, Canada with his wife and their animals.

www.ingramcontent.com/pod-product-compliance
Lightning Source LLC
Chambersburg PA
CBHW030336310726
48979CB00001B/60

* 9 7 8 1 9 1 3 7 6 6 4 0 5 *